FIRST LOVE

FIONA DAVENPORT

FIRST LOVE

Tucker Carrington knew what true, lasting love looked like. He grew up surrounded by it, but he never expected to feel it for himself when he was only twenty-one. Let alone for Eva Kendall, a girl he'd known since she was born. His best friend's sister.

Since Eva was too young for him, Tucker had to wait for the right moment to make her his. Heading overseas for his father's company, the distance didn't stop him from keeping an eye on Eva. Because she was his first—and forever—love.

PROLOGUE

TUCKER

"I'm going to kill Trevor! Ugh!!" Eva yelled as she stomped into the house and slammed the door. I leaned back in my chair and took a sip from my beer, keeping my eyes on the television screen. There was a game on, but I didn't have a fucking clue what it was or who was playing. My mind had been focused on waiting for Eva to return home from her date. She was home after only a couple of hours. Good

These days, I wanted to slap myself upside the head for thinking about her so much. Ever since my body started reacting to the womanly curves she'd developed, I tried not to. I was twenty-two, and she was only sixteen, but no matter how much I lectured myself on the fact that I was lusting after a kid—and my best friend's little sister, no less—my dick still stood at attention every time I saw her full tits, round hips, long legs, or heart-shaped ass.

Speaking of...Eva marched into the den, past where I was sitting, giving me a perfect view of that luscious ass. *Shit.* I looked at the ceiling and gulped down half my beer while thinking about Trevor in a bikini. Anything disgusting or boring to get my hard on to disappear.

Eva flipped her long, straight blond hair over her shoulder before putting her hands on her hips...*hairy legs, spiders, saggy breasts*...and stopped in front of her father, Justice. "Where the hell is my jerk of a brother?" she snapped.

"Language, baby girl," he said with a frown.

She sighed, "Sorry, Daddy. Do you know where my snot-nosed, butthead of a brother is?"

Justice's lips mashed together, clearly trying to suppress a smile, but the twinkle in his eyes gave away his amusement. "He's not home, Eva. Why?"

She huffed and threw her arms in the air. "My date was practically shaking in his boots when we left the house! He wouldn't touch me—he barely even looked at me the whole time we were out! Then he came up with some lame excuse to bring me home right after the movie when we were supposed to go to dinner."

I couldn't see her face, but it was clear that Justice's attempt to hide his glee at this news had failed when she folded her arms and stomped her foot. "Stop it, Daddy! This isn't funny! If Trevor doesn't stop scaring my dates, I'm going to die an old maid—and if you say one word about that being okay with you, I'm telling Mom."

That got him to wipe his expression clean real fast, and I had to fight not to laugh. Justice was one of my dad's best friends, so our families had spent a lot of time together growing up. Trevor and I found it hilarious that our fathers were completely whipped by their wives. Not that I blamed them. When my mom was mad at me, I went running in the opposite direction. Anything to avoid her wrath or, worse, her disappointment.

"I'll have a talk with him, baby girl," Justice promised. "Trevor will leave your dates alone from now on, okay?"

Eva bent down and threw her arms around her dad...*for fuck's sake, Tucker, get your mind and your eyes off this little girl's ass!* After she hugged him and gave him a kiss on the cheek, she stood and spun around. By the look of surprise on her face and the twin spots of pink that bloomed on her cheeks, she obviously hadn't noticed me before. "Hi, Tucker," she said softly, smiling sweetly. Her rosebud lips were plump, and no matter how hard I tried, I couldn't stop picturing them wrapped around my dick.

Fuck. Fuck. Fuck. It was a really good thing that I was leaving in a month. I needed to get away from temptation before I did something really stupid. It didn't help that I knew Eva had a crush on me. Unfortunately, my attempts to control myself around her often made me look like a complete asshole. Particularly when I made an effort to treat her like a kid—as a reminder to myself that she was off-limits.

I swallowed hard and managed to smile back without leering. I didn't want her dad catching on to my lust and kicking my ass from Manhattan to Connecticut. "Hey, Eva-bear." She gave me a cute little scowl at the use of the nickname I'd given her when she was six.

"I'm sixteen years old, Tucker. Don't you think it's time to start treating me like an adult?"

I snorted, earning another glare. "When you start acting like one, maybe I will."

Eva growled and stomped her foot in frustration.

I gestured to the floor and arched a brow. "Kinda proving my point there, Eva-bear."

She turned her head to look at her dad, probably expecting him to defend her, but he shook his head and smiled regretfully. "Sorry, baby girl. I'd rather you not grow up at all, so I'm not going to encourage it. And perhaps if you stopped dating punk-ass boys who aren't good enough for you...though I will tell Tucker to stop baiting you if that helps." Eva didn't hide her feelings for me very well, and I knew that while Justice hated to see his little girl hurt, he appreciated my attempts to quell her crush.

Eva threw her hands up in the air and let out a muted scream before pointing at Justice and snapping, "I'm telling Mom." Then she faced me again, the finger now pointing at me. "I don't know why you have to be such a jerk! And stop calling me Eva-bear!"

I shrugged and looked at the television, pretending I didn't give a shit about our conversation, when really, I was fighting the desire to grab her and run. "I'd agree, but it doesn't really matter. You won't be able to hear me call you that from London." Giving in to temptation, I glanced at her face in time to see it fall before she quickly smoothed out her expression.

FIONA DAVENPORT

"You're still moving next month?" she asked softly, her shoulders drooping.

"Yup." I returned my eyes to the television.

There was silence for a few moments, then I heard an almost inaudible sigh before her footsteps left the room.

"You know, Trevor left for Costa Rica last night." I turned my head and found Blair, Eva's mom, standing in the doorway.

Justice smiled at her with an innocent expression. "Did he?"

She stepped into the room and crossed her arms over chest, glaring at her husband. "You know very well he did, Justice Kendall. So who threatened Eva's date?"

My dad chose that moment to enter the room, and I silently applauded him for his timing. "What's the score?" he asked as he flopped down into another recliner facing the television and took a swallow from his beer.

Justice answered him before glancing back at Blair, his expression still innocent. She narrowed her eyes and stared at him for a moment before rolling her eyes. "We'll talk about this later."

After she was gone, Justice met my gaze and lifted his beer in a salute. I returned the gesture, and we both drained our bottles. It was his way of saying thank you. Not just for pushing Eva away, but because Trevor wasn't the one threatening the little assholes attempting to date Eva.

I was.

CHAPTER 1

TUCKER

My dad pulled me into a strong hug and pounded me on the back. "I'm so damn happy to have you home, son."

"Thanks, Dad." He let me go after a minute, and my mom's arms wrapped around me, squeezing me tight. Her head only came up to my shoulders, and I smiled as I bent my head to kiss the top of hers. "Hi, Mom." She sniffled, and I shook my head as I hugged her back. "Don't cry, Mom. You know we hate it when you cry."

"I'm just so happy to finally have my boy home," she replied as she let me go and stood back. She wiped under her eyes but smiled brightly, easing my discomfort at seeing my mom in tears.

"Tucker! Tucker! Tuuucker!" My youngest

sister, Hope, came racing down the hallway as fast as her seven-year-old legs would carry her. I squatted down and held open my arms with a giant smile on my face. She barreled into me, and I held her close as I shot to my feet and spun around.

"Hey, sunshine!" She squealed with joy, and the sound reminded me how much I'd missed my family for the past eight years. Hope had been a late surprise for my parents, fifteen years younger than my brother, Jackson. She'd been born shortly after I'd moved to England to head up a new European division in my dad's tech company. I'd been home on and off over the years but only for short visits. I couldn't stay long, or I would have given in to my desire to see Eva. And I knew that if I did, I wouldn't be able to leave again.

Now, my dad was ready to retire and was handing the company over to me completely, so I was finally back in New York to stay. And, this time, I wasn't going to keep my distance. I was going after the one I wanted, and I was going to make her mine.

I set my sister on her feet and kissed her forehead before straightening back up. She took my hand, and my dad threw an arm around my shoulders, both of them guiding me into the living room. I dropped down onto one of the couches in the large room, and

Hope curled up into my side. My little sister was adorable, and she reminded me of my goals. I wanted a family, and I was determined to start working on that right away.

"Are you sure you won't stay with us for a little while?" my mom asked as my dad pulled her down onto his lap.

"He's a grown man, Penelope," my dad said softly before brushing his lips over her temple. "He needs his own space." She pouted, and I almost caved. Only the reminder of my evening plans had me sticking to my guns.

"The work on my apartment was finished last week, and I'm anxious to get settled in my new home." I'd bought a three-level penthouse flat just off 5th Avenue on the Upper East Side near The Metropolitan Museum of Art. It was older and didn't have a great layout, so I'd had it gutted and completely renovated, specifically adding more bedrooms for a large family, and an art studio on the top floor. While drawing up the plans, I hacked Pinterest to see Eva's private boards in order to make sure she would be happy with all my choices. I was more than ready to settle down. I was anxious to get my woman home and get to work on breeding her.

My mom sighed but nodded with a smile. "I

understand. I won't guilt you into staying here. But I expect to see a lot of you, young man."

I laughed. "I promise."

We talked for a while, catching up on my siblings and the kids of my parents' friends who I'd grown up with. Eventually, my mom dragged Hope out of the room to get her ready for bed.

When I was alone with my dad, I decided to seek his advice on my situation. I knew a little about his and my mom's story. I was biologically my dad's nephew. When my parents had been killed, he'd taken me in and adopted me. Being a new dad, he'd felt out of his depth and had hired the girl next door to help him take care of his infant son. They'd fallen in love and married shortly after they met. My mom was over twenty years younger than my dad, but they were hopelessly in love, and it seemed as though their feelings had only grown over the years. I'd always known I wanted what they had, and I'd known who I wanted it with since I was twenty-one. But I hadn't fully accepted it until a few years after that. Then I'd spent the rest of my time away watching and preparing.

My dad was aware of what was going on because I'd eventually confided in him when I got tired of dealing with my obsession on my own. It wasn't like I could talk to Trevor about it. Facing Justice and Trevor were among the things that had driven me to seek my dad's advice. He'd shocked the hell out of me when he told me that I should go after what I wanted, no matter what, and that he would support me, even if it meant causing a rift between him and Justice. Dad had made a suggestion on the timing for that conversation, and I'd taken his advice. A couple of months before I was set to move back to New York, I'd flown home for one night, just to have a conversation with Justice and Trevor, in person, because I felt like I owed them that much.

Unlike my dad and Justice; his brother, Thatcher; and their mutual friend, Jamison, who'd all married and knocked up their wives before they were nineteen, I'd decided to wait until Eva was a little older. I'd definitely inherited the gene that made my woman my obsession, though. Only being a continent away had kept me from going after her before either of us were ready. Eva would never be happy living away from her family, and I'd needed those years in England to prepare for taking over for my dad. It had also given me the time I needed to make sure everything was ready and in place when I went for Eva.

And it had given Eva time to go to school

and get her dream job. Happily for me, it was a job she could continue during pregnancies and while raising our children. I'd also been pleased to see how many Pinterest boards she had that were centered around babies. It was clear she wanted a family too, so I didn't feel the slightest need to wait before I slid my fat cock into her unprotected womb and left my baby in there. And my sources had informed me that she didn't appear to be on any kind of birth control, so I was going to live in her pussy until my seed had taken root.

Which was why I'd scheduled a vacation before officially taking the reins from my dad. I'd also contacted Eva's boss and explained that I was her fiancé and requested leave for her so that I could surprise her with an elopement. Turned out, her boss was a romantic and couldn't agree fast enough. Things had fallen smoothly into place, and it was finally time to take action.

"I'm ready to go get her," I told my dad quietly.

He nodded and relaxed back into his chair, placing one ankle on the opposite knee. "I figured as much. You talked to her dad and brother?"

"Yes. I'm not sure either of them will be very happy with me for a while, but they gave me their blessing. Though I think Trevor will likely get over it faster than Justice."

My dad regarded me with a knowing gaze. "Trust me, when you have a daughter, you'll understand." Then he studied me for a moment before asking, "How much did you tell them?"

"Only that I want to marry Eva."

"Nothing about how you plan to convince her?"

I shrugged. "Nope." I didn't give a fuck what anyone thought about my methods because my focus was on taking and keeping Eva. And I would do whatever was necessary for that to happen. "I did make it clear that you know how I feel about her but didn't let on that you know about everything I've planned. So if they come to you after they find out, it's up to you whether to tell them."

"Tell who, what?" I almost jumped at the unexpected sound of my mom's voice. Her question had me freezing like a deer in headlights.

Okay, so I cared about one other person's opinion...which was why I'd kept my mom in the dark concerning Eva. I would tell her after I'd gotten my ring on my girl's finger. Hopefully, my mom wouldn't ever have to know what I did to get it there.

"Nothing, angel," my dad said as he stood and closed the distance between them. He grabbed her around the waist and dropped his head to kiss her. I appreciated his attempt to distract her, but when the kiss started to get out of hand, I wrinkled my nose and groaned.

"Seriously? I'm right here." I was used to my parents' PDA, but that didn't mean I wasn't going to complain about it. "I think five kids is more than enough proof that you do things I'd like to pretend you know nothing about. I don't need another reminder."

"I need to remember to give you shit when you bring your wife around someday and can't keep your hands to yourself," my dad mumbled against my mom's lips. She giggled, and I covered my face with my hands until the sounds of my dad mauling my mom stopped.

"Then I better be going so I can get myself that wife."

My mom laughed and rolled her eyes. "I'd like to see you bring home a date!" she teased. "Hard to find a wife without some of those." I could understand my mom's cynicism since I'd never brought a girl home before. But she didn't know the real extent of it...the truth was, I hadn't been on a date since I was a teenager. What was the point when I already knew they weren't going to measure up to the woman in my dreams?

Jumping to my feet, I strode over to my parents and pulled my mom from my dad's arms to mine. "You never know, Mom. I might surprise you." I winked at her and gave her a kiss on the cheek before letting her go and hugging my dad.

"Good luck," he murmured in my ear. I nodded in acknowledgment as I stepped away.

Hope popped into the room carrying a reusable grocery bag and handed it to me with a bright smile. I got down on one knee and looked inside to see that she'd packed me a goody bag. My sister loved to bake, and she was quite good at it, especially for a seven-year-old. "Are these some of your crazy-awesome treats, sunshine?" I gasped.

She clapped and bounced on her unicorn slippers. "Yes! We made them this morning just for you!"

Grinning, I pulled her into a hug. "Thank you, sunshine." She beamed at me, and I brought our faces close together before whispering, "I missed you most. Don't tell Mom." Then I held out my pinky, and she linked it with hers, shaking on the secret.

My parents' driver, Anthony, had come to pick

me up at the airport and had brought me straight to their house. My bags were still loaded in the Town Car, so I sent Anthony a text to let him know I was ready and gave a last round of hugs to everyone. With another promise to visit soon, I headed out to the car.

CHAPTER 2

TUCKER

*I*n London, I'd had the same house staff for almost the entire eight years I lived there. When I told them I was moving back to the States, I'd given all of them the choice to stay or go with me. I gave those who stayed a large severance package, but those who chose to relocate with me, I'd paid for their move and had my father's assistant—well, my assistant now—help to find them new housing. With the exception of Kendra Bay, my live-in housekeeper. No one could ever replace my mother, but Kendra had become a close second, so I was ecstatic when she agreed to come with me.

I sent my staff on ahead, and all of my belongings, except what was in my two suitcases, had been shipped to my flat the week before. I was certain that

Kendra had already unpacked everything. When I arrived at my new house, Kendra met me in the vestibule of the front elevator on the first floor of the flat. "Welcome home, Mr. Carrington."

With a warm smile, I pulled her into a hug and chuckled. "I'm so glad you're here, Kendra. And since when do you call me Mr. Carrington?"

She shrugged and winked as I released her. "Thought I'd give it a try."

"And what did you think?"

"Don't expect to hear it often, my boy," she said as she patted my cheek, making me laugh. "I've left dinner in the refrigerator. You just need to heat it in the oven. I also stocked the kitchen, including all the items on your list." She led me through the front door into the foyer, where I set down my suitcases, before following her to the left and through the dining room. We entered the large galley pantry that connected to the kitchen, and she showed me around the room so that I would be able to fend for myself and then gave me instructions on preparing the meal she'd left for me. She looked around and didn't seem to find anything else that needed to be addressed. "That's everything at the moment, I think. Now, since you gave me the night off, I'm going to get dolled up because I have a date."

Surprised by her announcement, I raised a brow. "A date? Who's this guy? I need to make sure he's good enough for you."

Kendra's cheeks pinkened, making me even more amused and curious. She patted her gray hair that was swept up into a bun and smoothed out some nonexistent wrinkles in her black pants. "His name is Anthony, and as I understand it, he works for your father."

I was speechless for a moment, but then I burst into laughter. Not because I thought it was a ridiculous idea, but because I couldn't believe I hadn't thought of how perfect they would be together before now. Both Kendra and Anthony were in their early fifties, widowed with grown children, and worked simply because retirement bored them. They were two of the best people I knew, and I wasn't at all surprised that they had hit it off. Obviously, they'd met when Anthony had been dispatched to pick up Kendra when she arrived.

"I approve," I told her when I'd stopped laughing. "But he better not try to steal you away from me." A grin split my face when I added, "Also, sleepovers are not discouraged or prohibited in your contract. And he wouldn't even have to do the walk of shame since you have your own elevator and entrance."

Kendra rolled her eyes and sniffed. "This is only our second date, Tucker. He has a ways to go before he earns his way into my knickers."

I snorted, and she glared at me before spinning around and marching through the kitchen door that led to her suite of rooms. I'd known Anthony for a long time, and I trusted him to treat Kendra right. But I made a mental note to have a "chat" with him about what would happen if he hurt her.

Still chuckling, I returned to the foyer for my suitcases. Then I took the elevator up to the third floor, which was comprised solely of the master suite, complete with a wraparound veranda and a sitting room that I'd had converted into an art studio. The elevator exited into another vestibule, and the door to the suite opened into a hallway. I headed left to unpack my bags in the bedroom. Once I was done, I explored the rest of the house so that I would be familiar enough to give Eva a thorough tour.

Returning to the bedroom, I took a quick shower, then I wrapped a towel around my waist and stood at the sink to trim my thin beard. Despite the fact that I was biologically related to my adopted father, I looked nothing like him or my adopted mom. I took after my birth mother with dark hair, tan skin, and brown eyes, though my six-foot-two height and muscular build came from the Carrington side of the family. I stayed in shape with regular workouts, but when I moved to England, I'd also taken up playing rugby. I even managed to find a league in New York so I could continue to play.

I'd been told I was easy on the eyes, but the only ones I was interested in were Eva's. The thought prompted me to check my watch, and I saw that it was nearing eight. I hurried my pace, wanting to arrive at my destination shortly after the hour. Once I'd dressed in black slacks with a black jacket and button-down shirt with an open collar, I grabbed my keys and wallet and headed out.

I took the elevator down to the building's garage and jogged over to my designated space where my Jag was parked. I'd considered using a driver, but I wanted to be alone with Eva, especially if she put up a fight. I hadn't seen her in person in eight years, and the last time, I'd hurt her feelings. I wasn't sure what kind of reception I was in for, but if she didn't come willingly, I wasn't above dragging her ass home and tying her to our bed. I had no doubt she would be screaming her forgiveness once I'd eaten her pussy a few times. I'd make sure she'd come around to my way of thinking before I popped her cherry and bred her.

As usual, traffic was a bitch, but I arrived at the small, Mediterranean restaurant in the Village at around half-past eight. *Who the fuck takes a date to this cheap hole in the wall?* I pulled into a parking garage conveniently located next door and slipped the attendant three hundred dollars to keep the car parked right in front of his booth. This way, I'd be able to get right in and drive out without waiting. The sooner the car was moving, the less time Eva would have to try to escape.

It hadn't taken me more than a few days in London to realize that I'd never survive the distance if I didn't have eyes or ears on Eva at all times and receive regular updates. And since I was very fucking good at what I did, I'd tapped Eva's cell phone and hacked all of her computers and accounts so I always knew what she was up to and continued to scare the hell out of any man she tried to date.

My access to her calendar was how I knew exactly when and where she would be tonight. I was immensely happy that this would be the last time I would need to send her date running. I probably could have waited until after...or taken her before, but this seemed much more entertaining.

I entered the restaurant and ignored the hostess's greeting as my gaze swept over the small space until it landed on the object of my obsession. My breath stalled in my lungs as I took her in. I had thousands and thousands of photos of Eva Kendal, but none of them had truly captured her beauty. Her long, white-blond hair was swept up into some kind of knot on the back of her head. I immediately decided I was going to pull it down pin by pin while she sucked my cock. She was facing the windows just to my left, so I had a clear view of her bright blue eyes, button nose, and full, rosebud lips. She was wearing a long-sleeved, straight green dress that fell past her knees and low-heeled pumps. I felt an arrogant grin stretch across my face. Her outfit clearly conveyed that this night would not be ending with sex. Well...not with the dickhead sitting across from her anyway. I was going to peel that nun-like dress from her body slowly, licking every inch of skin as it was exposed.

My dick was hard as a baseball bat, and for the first time, I didn't bother to try to hide it. Let her date see what he was losing to. He was a thin guy of medium height and had muddy brown hair that I could tell from the side was slicked back from his face. I was confident in my assumption that he was probably equipped with a pee-wee bat, versus my major league cock.

I knew Eva was a virgin and hadn't seen this asshole's pecker—*she better not have or I'm going to kill the son of a bitch*. Still, it didn't stop me from wanting to prove that I was more man than this guy would ever be. It would be pretty obvious once she saw the monster between my legs.

Eva smiled at something he said, and my lips dropped into a frown. I didn't want her smiles being directed at anyone but me from now on. It was time to get this bullshit over with. The hostess again tried to get my attention, but I just waved her off as I marched over to Eva's table.

I stopped when I was right in front of it, standing between the two occupants. My eyes were glued to my gorgeous girl as I crooned, "Hello, Eva-bear."

She froze for a second before her head flew up and to the side, meeting my gaze. Surprise flitted in her blue pools, then bright joy and a flash of desire before it was quickly snuffed out and replaced with irritation. "What the hell are you doing here, Tucker?"

I raised a brow and touched a finger to her bottom lip before tracing them both. "Don't dirty this pretty mouth with language like that, baby," I scolded softly, an undercurrent of warning in my tone.

"Excuse me, we're on a date!" The pipsqueak sitting opposite my girl dragged my attention away, his nasal voice immediately grating on my nerves.

I swung my head his way, and the violent scowl on my face had his draining of all color while he shrank back in his seat. "Leave," I commanded.

I didn't react to Eva's gasp, keeping my eyes trained on the little shit as he swallowed hard. "Who do you think you are?" he asked, his voice cracking from the effort it was obviously taking him to try to be brave. It was a wasted effort because my hand shot out to grasp the knot of his tie and lift him to his feet as he sputtered and choked.

"Don't make me tell you again," I snarled. When I let go, he stumbled backward before running to the door like his ass was on fire. I shook my head and took his seat, stretching my legs out sideways from the chair and returning my gaze to my woman. Damn, she was so sexy in her prim and proper little getup. I'd known Eva all her life, and I knew what kind of fire she was hiding beneath the boring façade. I wondered if she would mind if I ripped it off her delectable body.

"Tucker!" Eva snapped, drawing me out of my

thoughts. "What the hell was that?"

I narrowed my eyes and mimicked her tone. "Language, Eva."

"Don't tell me..." She broke off and rolled her eyes to the ceiling. "You know what? Forget it." Her chin dropped forward, and she stared at me with a mixture of anger and curiosity. "Seriously, what are you doing here?"

The hostess chose that moment to approach our table, keeping me from responding right away. She leaned down much farther than necessary to place a menu in front of me. Her tits were practically falling out of the deep V of her shirt. I grimaced and just barely restrained the impulse to gag at the cloud of perfume surrounding her. When she straightened, my eyes returned to Eva, and I smirked at the daggers she was shooting toward the obnoxious woman. Jealousy looked hot as fuck on my girl. And it strengthened my belief that it wouldn't take much to bring her around to my way of thinking.

When the hostess finally left, I smiled and leaned over the table, reaching a hand out to draw a single digit from her temple to her jaw. "I've come for you, Eva-bear."

She squeezed her lids shut for a beat and sighed. "I'm twenty-four years old, Tucker. Stop calling me that!" Her voice had risen at the end of her demand, and she quickly glanced around to see if she'd disturbed anyone. I was sure plenty of the patrons were paying attention, but they were all pretending to be engrossed in their food.

"It doesn't matter how old you are, baby. You'll always be my Eva-bear."

She screwed up her face and rose from her seat, then came to stand in front of me. She crossed her arms under her ample tits and the action pushed them up, making my mouth water. "Great, did you come here just to tell me that you will always see me as a child?" she growled adorably.

My eyes drifted to the top of her head before slowly traveling down, taking in every one of her features until they'd reached her toes. "Just because I call you by a nickname I gave you when you were a child doesn't mean I don't see the sexy, grown-up woman standing in front of me." I looked up to see her mouth slightly open, and her eyes rounded with shock. Grabbing her hips, I dragged her between my legs. I loved how round and wide they were, perfect for carrying my babies. I also couldn't fucking wait to hold those curves in my hands while I buried my cock in her pussy over and over again.

Her tits were right at eye level, but I succeeded

in keeping my attention on her face, though it was extremely difficult. "Now, let's get back to my reason for being here."

She frowned and cocked her head to the side. "What do you mean, you're here for me?" Her eyes narrowed in suspicion. "Did my dad send you? Or Trevor?"

My hands stayed on her hips as I planted my feet on the ground and pushed up out of the chair. Then I slid them up her sides, allowing my thumbs to brush along the undersides of her breasts and smiled when I felt her tiny shiver. I ended their exploration at her neck, wrapping my hands around it and forcing her chin up with my thumbs. "No, Eva-bear. I meant exactly what I said. I've come for you. No one sent me, and no one is going to stop me from taking you."

My gorgeous girl inhaled sharply and tried to shake her head, but my firm grip stopped the movement. "T-taking me?" she sputtered. Something in her eyes clued me into the fact that she had picked up on my double entendre but wasn't sure if I'd meant it.

I nodded and dropped my eyes to the large bulge straining against the zipper of my pants. When I looked up at her again, I was satisfied that her gaze had followed mine because she was still staring at my cock. "You're mine, Eva-bear. And I'm taking you in every way possible."

Eva gaped at me and opened her mouth, but before she could say anything, the damn hostess was intruding again. "Sir, is there anything you need? I can—"

I would never hit a woman, but I did give her the same deadly glare I'd leveled on Eva's "date." She stumbled back a few steps, almost toppling over on her ridiculously high heels. Although they looked trashy on her, I admitted to myself that I would love to feel them digging into my back as I fucked Eva fast and hard.

If my dick got any bigger, it was going to rip a hole in my three-thousand dollar, custom-tailored dress pants, trying to get to Eva. I was tired of having an audience and was practically vibrating with my need for her. It was time to get the fuck out of there before I dragged her to the bathroom and took her like an animal.

I glowered at the hostess, and she squeaked as she hurried back to the front of the restaurant. Then I turned and threw some money on the table before scooping Eva into my arms and stalking out the front door.

CHAPTER 3

TUCKER

Eva was silent as I carried her out the door to my waiting car. Surprised at her lack of reaction, I glanced down at her face and almost laughed. She was glaring at me as though she was trying to murder me with her eyes. It was so fucking cute, all I wanted to do was press her up against the nearest wall and kiss the hell out of her.

However, it could wait until I had her safely ensconced in our home. The attendant tossed me my keys, and I caught them with the hand behind Eva's back. He opened the passenger side door, and I started to thank him when I noticed him eyeballing Eva's chest. I practically growled, startling him, and when he clocked my expression, he went running back to his booth.

I placed Eva in her seat and swiftly pulled the seat belt across her, clicking it into place. Then I slammed the door shut and hit the lock button as I jogged around the front of the Jag. I used the key to open the door and dropped into the driver's seat. Eva had just managed to unfasten her seat belt, and I shot my arm out to grab it and fasten it once more.

"Fine," she grumbled. "You can take me home."

"You read my mind, Eva-bear," I chuckled.

"Are you planning on scaring everyone to death?" she snipped a minute later.

I laughed and shook my head, yet my voice was firm when I answered, "Only the ones who can't keep their eyes off what's mine. Or interfere with my plans."

"Yours?" she repeated quietly.

I gave her a hard look. "Mine."

To my surprise, she was quiet after that. Until I approached 65th Street, where her apartment was located, several blocks to the east. "You can turn here," she informed me with a wave of her right hand. I continued straight and saw her turn her head toward me out of the corner of my eye. "Or 68th." Which was the next street that went east.

When I passed that one too, she twisted her whole body in my direction, and I glanced over to see her scrutinizing me. "I thought you were taking me home."

I nodded as I looked back to the road. "I am."

"Where exactly do you think my home is?" she asked, her tone exasperated.

"You'll see, baby. Be patient."

"Be patient? You're practically kidnapping me, Tucker!"

I stifled a grin and shrugged. "Not practically," I explained in a pleasantly neutral tone as though we were discussing the weather. "That's exactly what I'm doing."

Eva gasped and reared back, bumping into the door. "What the fuck are you talking about?" she shouted.

My head whipped around, and I scowled at her. "Watch your mouth, Eva."

Her eyes narrowed, and she squared her shoulders defiantly. "Or what, Tucker?"

I was forced to focus on the road once more as I approached 80th Street and our home. So I added extra steel to my tone when I answered since she wouldn't be able to see the serious expression on my face. "Or I'll spank that pretty ass of yours until you feel my handprint on both cheeks for days." The image sent a shockwave of lust from my brain, straight to my cock.

"I-I don't—" she sputtered. "I don't even know what to say to that."

I shrugged and turned into the driveway that tunneled down into the underground garage. "We're here," I declared as I brought the car to a stop in my space. I was out of the Jag and around to her side in a flash, yet she'd still managed to unbuckle and hop out of the car. She took one step in the direction of the garage exit, but that was as far as she got before I grabbed her waist and flung her up and over my shoulder. Eva struggled until I planted a resounding slap on her ass. "Stop it, Eva. You're going to hurt yourself." Then I swallowed a groan. Fuck. I nearly came when my hand had landed on the globe. Damn, her ass was luscious, big and round, and I was anxious to see it jiggle as I rutted in her from behind. I knew she would earn herself another spanking, which made me grin because I longed to see my pink handprint on her lily-white skin.

She gasped in outrage, and I rolled my eyes. She could pretend that hadn't turned her on, but I'd felt the shiver that coursed through her body. And with her over my shoulder, the succulent aroma of her arousal filled my nostrils. Like Eva, I had no experience with sex and had never smelled a woman's desire, but somehow, I knew that Eva's scent was better than anything I would have encountered had I not waited for her.

"Put me down this instant, Tucker Carrington. You can't just kidnap me!" She was shouting, probably hoping someone would hear her. Too bad for her; we'd entered the vestibule to my private elevator, and it was soundproofed.

I was tempted to give her another love tap on her juicy ass but decided to save it for later. We had a long night ahead of us, and it would only fuel my hunger, making it harder to be patient while I explained things to Eva.

The elevator door swished open after I pressed my fingerprint on the scanner, and I carried her inside. Once the doors shut and we were ascending, I slowly lowered her to her feet, keeping her body snug against mine. Just before she touched the ground, the hard bulge of my cock dragged along her pussy, and we both moaned. I dropped my head back against the wall with a thump and closed my eyes, praying for control. Eva cleared her throat and tried to step away, but I palmed her ass and held her in place while I breathed deep and even.

Finally, I felt like I had a better grip on myself

and opened my eyes to gaze down at the precious woman in my arms. She was looking everywhere but at me, and her cheeks were aflame with a bright blush. I snickered, causing her to glare as her eyes returned to my face.

"See what you do to me, baby?" I murmured, lowering my head until our lips were centimeters apart.

The elevator stopped and opened before she had a chance to reply. With a sigh of regret, I allowed her to take two steps back, but I took hold of her hand and entwined our fingers together. Then I took the lead and guided her across the small atrium and through the front door. I hung a right and ushered her into the massive living room that had large windows with a view of Central Park and The Metropolitan Museum of Art.

Eva's eyes were like saucers as she took everything in. She blinked owlishly and her mouth had formed a wide O. "This is your apartment?" she inquired with quiet awe.

I almost corrected her that it was, in fact, *our* home but decided it could wait until after we'd gone over some other things. "I bought it several months ago and had it completely renovated to fit a large family. There are plenty of bedrooms to fill on the second floor and a larger space that I thought could be used as a playroom. I also added a new feature that I thought would specifically please my wife."

She'd been standing in front of one of the giant windows, but at my words, she spun around, her face a mask of astonishment. "You're getting married?" she croaked. She wrapped her arms around herself and shrunk back against the glass. "Then why did you bring me here? Am I a game to you? One last fling before you get tied down?"

Shit. I hadn't expected her mind to go running off in the wrong direction. I held out my hand and beckoned her. "Come here, Eva-bear." She shook her head, and I frowned. "You are not a game, a fling, or any other ridiculous thing that would make you less than what you are to me. Now get your little ass over here. I'm going to explain everything, but I won't do it with you cowering across the room."

As I suspected, my use of the term "cowering" needled her, and she bristled, quickly standing at attention and squaring her shoulders. She stomped over to me, and I immediately yanked her into my body, spun around, and pressed her into the wall, anchoring my hands on both sides of her head before slamming my mouth down over hers.

CHAPTER 4

TUCKER

Fuck, yes, I thought with a low groan. I finally had my lips on my woman, and she was even sweeter than I'd imagined. Eva sucked in a breath, and I took advantage of it, slipping my tongue inside her mouth and rubbing it against hers. She moaned, and it was the sweetest sound, going straight to my dick and causing it to leak. I moved in closer and dropped my hands to her shoulders as I crowded her until there was no space between us.

I angled my head for deeper access, and her tits rubbed on my chest as her breathing sped up. Her nipples poked through her dress, and my fingers itched to touch them. I gave in to my need and glided my hands down until I was cupping her big, soft globes. She moaned when I gently squeezed them and brushed my thumbs over the hard peaks. She was so fucking responsive. Her nipples tightened even more as I teased them, her body pressing into mine as though she couldn't get close enough, and her tongue danced and twisted seamlessly with mine as though we'd done this a million times.

Eventually, I needed more, and I moved my arms around her, dropping my hands to cup her ass and lifting her off her feet so that our groins were perfectly aligned. My hips bucked, and Eva cried out as her legs flew around my waist. "Fuck," I rasped. "You feel so good, baby." I dragged my lips along her jaw up to her ear and whispered, "Are you wet for me, Eva?" She didn't respond fast enough for my liking, and I thrust into her again before biting her earlobe hard enough to cause a sting.

"Yes!" she cried out.

"Yes, what?"

She pulled back and glared at me, though the effect was somewhat ruined by the fiery passion burning in her eyes. "I'm wet for you, Tucker. Fucking soaked. Are you happy?"

Glaring right back at her and holding her tight, I pivoted and stalked over to one of the couches. I set her on her feet before dragging her down with me as

I sat. Before she knew what was happening, I'd draped her over my knee and shoved up her skirt.

"What are you—!" Eva exclaimed, but I cut her off.

"I warned you about your language, Eva," I growled. She lifted her head and turned it to the side to stare at me with disbelief. I glared at her before gazing down at what I'd uncovered. I swallowed hard when I saw two bare cheeks staring back at me. *Fucking hell.* My cock was past its breaking point, and I came a little in my pants as I spotted the lacy tops of her thigh-high stockings, her black garter belt, and the black line of lace that disappeared between her milky-white cheeks.

I raised a hand and as I brought it down, my cock released another burst of come. More than likely, my pants were ruined, but I didn't have one fuck to give about it. I slapped the opposite side, mesmerized by the way it made her ass jiggle. I paused when I heard a small sound from Eva. It had been so quiet I'd almost missed it. I spanked each cheek again, listening carefully this time, and I was rewarded when she moaned a little louder this time.

I slipped a hand between her legs and drew a finger through her slit. She was beyond drenched, and when I lifted my hand, her juices were dripping from my finger. I popped it in my mouth and leaked even more come as I licked the digit clean. She tasted like sugar and honey, and I was suddenly starving. I resumed spanking her luscious ass and stopped frequently to finger her pussy for another taste of her ambrosia. The harder I brought my hand down, the more liquid gushed from her center. Finally, I was satisfied to see that the pink color from where I'd spanked her wasn't fading. I grunted in approval, knowing she would feel her punishment every time she sat down the following day. Then my eyes rolled to the back of my head as the sight had another burst of come spewing from my steel rod.

I'd waited over eight years to have Eva in my arms, to taste her, to feel her beneath me, experience her coming around me. The feeling was almost too much, and it took every ounce of my determination to do this right to keep from saying fuck it and taking her straight to the bedroom. With the way she was responding to me, I knew it wouldn't take much to convince her.

Drawing in a deep breath and sending up a prayer for control, I smoothed Eva's skirt back down into place. Then I lifted her and turned her to straddle my lap. I almost smiled at her dark scowl. It was adorable. But my cock was pissed at being left hanging, and from the state of her flushed skin and rapid breathing, I guessed that was the reason for her too.

"Are you kidding me, Tucker Carrington?" she seethed.

I raised an eyebrow and gave her my most innocent expression.

"I can't believe you spanked me!"

I cocked my head to the side and stared at her, a verbal reminder of why she was punished seemed unnecessary.

"You can't tell me how to talk," she grumbled. "You don't own me."

Now I was the one glaring. "Don't push me, Eva-bear. Or you might earn yourself another spanking."

She huffed and wiggled on my lap, forcing me to swallow a groan. "You could have at least let me finish."

I was right. "You come when I tell you, baby. And it wouldn't be much of a punishment if you enjoyed it. Now would it?"

"Arrgh!!" Eva punched me in the shoulder and tried to scramble off my lap, but I held her hips firmly, keeping her right where I wanted her. Well, I really wanted her in my bed with her legs spread and my head buried in her pussy. But we'd get to that later.

"I think it's time to get some things straight, Eva," I informed her in a low, commanding voice.

She folded her arms and quietly fumed, but she'd stopped trying to get away, so I continued.

"I waited until you were of age. Until you'd finished school and established a career for yourself. I was patient while you continued to date assholes, forcing me to threaten their lives if they came near you again." She gasped, and I could tell she was about to yell, so I covered her mouth and kept speaking. "Eight long fucking years I've waited for you, watched you, protected you. So don't tell me you don't belong to me, Eva. You've been mine since you were fifteen years old, and I think, deep down, you've known it."

"How would I know any such thing, Tucker?" she snapped, but I didn't miss the hint of sadness in her eyes. It made my heart ache for what I'd put her through even though it had been necessary. "You barely knew I existed when I was a kid, you were mean to me when I was a teenager, and I haven't seen more than an occasional picture of you in my entire adult life."

I dragged the pads of my fingers along her

jawline. "I know, baby. But trust me, I was always aware of you. You were just so fucking young when you started to become a woman. I couldn't handle it. Especially once it became clear that you had a crush on me. And I knew if I didn't stay away..." I shook my head and gave her a regretful smile. I'd done what was right, but that didn't mean I didn't hate myself for hurting her. "I was never far from you, despite being an ocean away."

Eva licked her lips, and I watched her tongue with jealous fascination. I wanted my tongue to be the only one that tasted those pink lips. "I don't understand," she said quietly, drawing my attention away from her mouth.

I sighed and shifted on the couch, unable to find a comfortable position, particularly with the woman of my dreams sitting on my lap. My restlessness might also have had something to do with the fact that I'd almost revealed just how deep my obsession with her ran. I couldn't risk showing my hand until she was tied to me so tightly that it wouldn't scare her away. "I promise to explain everything later. But right now, I'm just going to lay out the important facts." I took her chin between my thumb and index finger, holding her in an iron grip so she was forced to keep her eyes on my face.

I wanted her to see how serious I was about what I had to say next.

"You belong to me, Eva Kendal." My other hand squeezed one of her butt cheeks. "This pink ass is mine." I released her behind and brought my hand up to cup one of her generous breasts. "These tits are mine." I traced her mouth with one finger. "These lips." My neck bent, and I kissed her hard before pulling back to meet her eyes again. "All of you. Your body. Your heart. Mine." The last word came out in a growl, and her eyes simmered with heat until she seemed to realize what she was giving away and shuttered her expression.

"You can't just decide that I'm yours," she sputtered. There wasn't much conviction behind her words, and I decided the time for talking was over. I needed to get her naked and working on getting her bred. Not only so she could never leave me, but because I wanted a big family and the image of Eva round with my baby had me on the verge of jizzing in my pants like a fucking teenager.

"Your body says otherwise, baby," I grunted and brought our faces mere centimeters apart. "The way you gushed all over my hand while I was stroking your pussy was proof of that."

I held her body firmly to mine as I surged to my

feet. She opened her mouth and started to mumble a denial, but I crushed my mouth over hers. It wasn't far to get to the stairs, and I only bumped into one wall on the way since I couldn't see much while I was ravishing her lips, sucking on her tongue, and making sure that every step I took rubbed her hot center against my raging dick. Fearing I would trip and hurt her, I tore my mouth from hers and jogged up to the third floor as fast as possible, so she didn't have time to break out of the daze my kiss had left her in.

At the top of the steps, I returned to devouring her as I stumbled down the hall to the master bedroom. Once we were through the door, I turned and shoved her up against the wall, too impatient to make it to the bed just yet. My hips held her in place while my hands went around her back. One slipped up to pull the pins from her hair and the other found the zipper to her dress and yanked it down. I pulled back just enough to let the top of the dress fall forward. Eva's tits were spilling out of the black lace cups of her bra, the tops jiggling with each heaving breath. It reminded me of what was underneath her outwardly modest outfit.

I needed to see her. All of her.

I took one step back, enough to drop her feet to

the floor, then I dragged the dress down until it was loose enough to fall to the floor by itself. Then I took another step back and admired the vision before me.

Her big tits made my mouth water, the hard nipples poking through the lace. Her stomach was flat—I'd be changing that as soon as possible—her hips flared, leading to long legs that were encased in nude silk that started at the tops of her thighs and were held up by black lace. Last, my gaze landed at the apex of her legs, and I groaned when I saw how wet her panties were.

My girl had a naughty streak. A seductress hidden under an innocent's clothes. It was a perfect mixture of sweet and spicy. A thought suddenly entered my mind, and I stiffened for a moment, before my arms shot out and I gripped Eva's shoulders. "Who were you wearing this sexy as fuck underwear for, Eva?" I growled. It better not have been for that fucker she'd been having dinner with. "Were you expecting someone to peel away your innocent disguise to discover the vixen you were hiding beneath it?" My stare bored into her as the thought of another man seeing or touching what was mine had a murderous rage building inside me.

Eva looked a little frightened. I was sure she could see the anger pouring off me. I didn't want to scare her, but she needed to realize that I would put any motherfucker in the ground who made the mistake of getting too close to my woman. "No," she whispered.

"Then explain to me why you're wearing it."

She lowered her lashes for a few moments before looking back up at me through them. Pink bloomed on her cheeks, the color matching the shade I'd left painted on her ass. If I hadn't been so focused on her answer, it might have snapped the last threads of my control. "I wear it because it makes me feel sexy. Even though no one knows it's there but me."

I nodded, letting her know her answer was acceptable. Relief trickled through my veins, slowly dousing the burning rage, but it was quickly replaced with an even more potent hunger. My hands glided over her collarbones and down to mold around her breasts. I dipped a finger below the fabric on each one and brushed the pads over her taut nipples. She sucked in a breath, and I smiled at the proof of my effect on her. I slid my palms down her sides and traced the top of her garter belt before they skated around her back to palm her naked ass. "One day, I'm going to fuck you in a getup like this," I vowed . "But tonight, I need to see you. To finally see your gorgeous body in person." Shit. My eyes shot to her face to see if she'd picked up on my slip of the tongue. Yeah, it probably made me an incredible asshole, but when I said I always had eyes on her, I meant it.

Eva looked dazed, and I doubted she was clear-headed enough to pick up on my subtle confession. I grunted as I squeezed her ass before moving down to her thighs and using a strong grip to hoist her up. Her legs automatically circled my waist and she locked them, cradling my cock snugly against her pussy. I could feel the heat through three layers of clothing and my dick was practically weeping with the need to bury itself inside her.

CHAPTER 5

TUCKER

I mentally lectured my cock about wasting come as I hurried over to the massive bed situated on the wall opposite large windows that looked out over the veranda and Central Park. The views from our apartment were amazing, but I only had eyes for the beauty I was slowly lowering to the ground. I gently pushed her chest until she fell back onto the mattress with her legs hanging over the side. After ditching my shirt—meaning I tore it off, sending the buttons flying everywhere—and quickly stripping out of my pants, I licked my lips and dropped to my knees. Grasping the top of the garter belt, I dragged it off, along with her panties and stockings. Then I put my hands on her knees and spread her open for me.

Holy fucking shit. I'd never in my life seen anything as beautiful and mouthwatering as Eva's bare, pink, glistening pussy. She tried to close her legs, and I growled in warning as I firmly widened them again, using my shoulders to keep her in place. I skimmed a single digit up through her slit, and when it came away covered in sticky cream, I licked it clean with a hum of pleasure. "You taste so fucking incredible, baby," I groaned as I dived in to drink her nectar straight from the source. Eva cried out when I sucked her hard little clit into my mouth and bit down lightly.

I devoured her pussy, licking and sucking every inch of her drenched sex. My stiffened tongue plunged into her virgin hole, and her walls closed around it as she screamed. I feasted on her pussy without pausing even as I frantically used one hand to yank down my zipper and liberate my cock from its prison, almost sighing as the pain eased somewhat. Without the distraction of my zipper biting into my flesh, I was able to give my sweet girl all of my attention.

My tongue fucked her tight channel a few more times before I dragged it up to her clit and replaced it with one finger. Damn, she was snug. A heady rush of power and possession coursed through my body when I felt the thin barrier of her virginity. I knew she hadn't been with anyone, but for some reason, feeling the proof for myself made me want to roar and bang my chest like a caveman. "Did you save this pussy for me, baby?"

She could deny it if she wanted, but I'd known from her first reaction to me at the restaurant that she hadn't gotten over me. It had been clear as day that she still harbored feelings for me. Even if I'd only glimpsed them for a moment before she shut out her emotions. Now, I wanted to hear her admit it.

I stopped the movement of my finger inside her and looked up. "Eva? I can feel that you're untouched, baby. But I want to hear you say it. Tell me you saved your cherry just for me."

Her head lifted so she could see me as she brought herself up onto her elbows. Blue eyes stared at me, cloudy with desire even as wariness drifted through them. My tongue darted out to lick around her clit while I waited for her to respond. She shivered, and the muscles in her thighs quaked. "Answer me, Eva," I demanded. She bit her lip, and I growled, frustrated that I had no way to suck on both her lips at the same time. I silently cursed her teeth like a complete madman. Who was jealous of teeth?

Eva's eyes slid away from mine, and her flushed

skin still couldn't hide the blush that bloomed on her face. I knew she was about to deny it, and I scowled. "Don't lie to me, baby," I snarled, my tone packed with warning.

"I haven't met anyone that made me want to let them take me to bed," she murmured.

I arched a brow and pierced her with a steady gaze. "Anyone? Or anyone since me?"

Eva frowned but fell back onto the bed with a moan when I licked up her center with the flat of my tongue and sucked hard on her bundle of nerves. "Yes. Anyone since you," she admitted with a ragged sigh.

"Good girl, baby," I praised her softly before diving back in to finish what I started. I didn't draw it out any longer, wanting to reward her for being honest and because I was at the end of my rope. I scissored my fingers inside her, stretching her before adding a third. I was big everywhere, and I wanted to prepare her tight pussy for the invasion of my long, thick cock. A few minutes later, she began to shake and cry out.

"Please, Tucker," she begged, "Please let me come!"

Her pleas went straight to my dick, making it throb in time with the pulse in her pussy. I sped up my ministrations and pushed her over the edge until she tumbled into a shattering orgasm and screamed my name.

I licked her one last time, then wiped my face on her thigh before getting to my feet. My eyes devoured her as I stripped off the rest of my clothes. Then I lifted her and gently moved her to the center of the bed. Precome dripped from the tip of my angry cock onto her stomach as I placed my knees on both sides of her thighs. Her breathing was beginning to even out, but her tits were still straining against the lacy bra with her every breath. I made a mental note to send a million dollars to the person who invented the bra with the front closure.

With one twist of my fingers, the clasp gave way, and her breasts spilled out. The big mounds were milky white with rosy tips. "You are so fucking beautiful, baby," I breathed. As I gazed down at them, I could imagine what they'd look like when they were even more swollen and dripping with milk. "You have the perfect tits for feeding our babies. I can't wait to see them heavy and full." I swallowed hard. "It makes me thirsty." I swooped down to wrap my lips around one nipple and groaned when Eva gasped and arched her back, shoving more of her breast into my mouth. My hands were splayed on her rib cage, and they drifted up to frame her tits, holding them up as I laved attention on each one in turn. Eva moaned and writhed, her fingers clutching my hair as though she was afraid I would stop. Not fucking happening.

When I had my fill, I trailed kisses down to her stomach and placed a soft lingering one there. Then I moved over her and took her lips, drinking deeply as I spread her legs and settled between them. My cock slid between her slick folds, and I groaned as the heat of her pussy bathed my tip.

A thought split through the haze of lust filling my brain, and I jerked my head back. "You're not on anything, are you?" I growled with eyes narrowed on her face.

Her eyes widened, and she shook her head. "Shit! Do you have a condom?" Her hands pushed against my chest, but I was immovable.

"No, baby. And I'm not using one with you," I stated, my tone brooking no argument. I pushed in an inch, and her eyes closed as she moaned. "I'm popping your sweet little cherry bare."

"You—you have to pull out—" She broke off and gasped when I pulled her legs around my waist and pushed in until I bumped into her thin barrier.

I dreaded the next part, but I was determined to

get everything I'd ever wanted, and that meant breaching Eva's maidenhead. I touched my forehead to hers and whispered, "I'm so sorry I have to hurt you, baby." My hands wrapped around her fleshy hips, and I crushed my mouth on hers as I surged forward until I was balls deep in her virgin pussy. "Fuck!" I roared, completely shaken by the ecstasy that washed over my body.

I just barely managed to keep from coming as I locked myself in place. Tears leaked from the edges of her eyes, and I kissed each one as I waited for her to stretch and accommodate my long, thick cock.

After a couple of minutes, I felt her begin to relax, and I exhaled the breath I hadn't realized I'd been holding. I brushed a soft kiss over her lips as I tested her by circling my hips. She moaned into my mouth, and her legs tightened around me.

This time, I pulled almost all of the way out before slamming back in. Eva threw her head back and screamed as her walls clamped down on me like a vise. "Shit," I grunted. "You feel so damn good, baby. I knew it would be like this between us. And knowing this pussy will only ever know the feel my cock is making it really fucking hard not to lose control."

I started a steady rhythm, fighting the tight grip

her pussy had on my cock. "Tucker," she cried out, her head thrashing from side to side.

"I fucking love hearing my name from your lips." Tingling sparked at the base of my spine, and my balls felt heavy and full. I wasn't going to last much longer; I was already spilling small amounts of come with every thrust. But I wouldn't let go until she was in the throes of an orgasm so that her womb was ripe and open.

My hand shot out to snatch a pillow, and I quickly shoved it under her hips. I didn't want to chance any of my seed slipping out. The new angle sent me even deeper with the next thrust. Eva's whole body shuddered, and she hissed, "Yes! Don't stop, Tucker."

"Never, my love," I rasped. Rising to my knees, I watched my cock disappear and reappear, shiny with her arousal. "I need you to come, Eva," I growled. "Now."

She'd begun to cry out with every slam of my hips, so I placed the pad of my thumb on her clit and rubbed it in circles. "Shit!" she yelped.

"Language!" I snapped. I pulled out and slapped her pussy before slamming back in. Eva's body tensed, and her breath caught seconds before she screamed and flew apart.

I planted myself as deep as possible and shouted as my orgasm shot down my spine and exploded out of my cock. "Eva!"

Her pussy milked my shaft in strong pulses, sucking up each jet of come. "That's it, baby," I groaned. "Take it all. Every drop." I continued to gently thrust, dragging out her orgasm and making sure to push my seed in as far as I could.

When my tremors began to subside, I was sapped of my strength. And though I wanted to stay inside Eva forever, I fell onto my side. Cuddling her close, I threw an arm and a leg over her and sighed with contentment.

CHAPTER 6

TUCKER

"Tucker!"

My eyes dragged open when I felt a small punch on my shoulder and Eva's voice saying my name. Her tone wasn't happy and satisfied like I expected it to be. Instead, she sounded almost angry. My lips curved down in a frown when I spotted her hovering over me, her eyes narrowed in an accusing glare.

I curled my arm around her waist and gently brought her down so she was lying over my chest. Then I kissed the crown of her head and sighed, dead tired from getting almost no sleep the night before. "What's on your mind, Eva-bear?" It was morning, and the sun was shining brightly through the windows of our bedroom, causing me to squint as I looked down at her face.

"How can you be so calm?" she shrieked as she tried to push off me. I kept my arms banded around her like steel, holding her against my body. I wasn't about to let her go in this state. Chasing her ass down was not on my to-do list for the day. The majority of the list had to do with pampering my girl and continuing the mission to breed her. "You promised you would pull out!"

My eyes snapped open, and I was suddenly wide-awake as I stared at her with mild surprise. "And when do you imagine I did that?" I asked. I'd filled her pussy over and over the night before, so I wasn't sure why she was just freaking out about this now.

She huffed but didn't try to pull away again. I assumed it was because she knew the attempt would be pointless. "I told you I wasn't on birth control, and you needed to pull out and you—" I cocked an eyebrow and she paused, then her skin flushed, making my cock harden. "You didn't—"

I shook my head emphatically. "I will never lie to you, baby. And I think I made it pretty clear last night that you are mine. Nor did I try to hide the fact that it's my intention to put my baby inside you."

Eva's mouth dropped open, and I licked my lips. I was definitely going to have her on her knees at some point today.

"B-but you c-can't," she sputtered.

I sat up and maneuvered her to straddle my lap, fighting a groan when her wet pussy hugged my rapidly growing dick and then narrowed my eyes. "The fuck I can't," I growled. "I have waited eight long years to claim you as mine. And I'm going to make sure that every last person on earth knows it by putting a huge fucking rock on your pretty little finger and a sexy little bump in your belly."

Eva stared at me for a moment and then swallowed hard—the image of her swallowing like that while my cock was down her throat made it nearly impossible to concentrate on our discussion. "Eight years?" she parroted.

I nodded without severing the connection between our eyes.

"But you...you hated me." Her eyes glistened with moisture, and my heart cracked.

I cupped her cheeks and spoke in a firm, though regretful tone. "Never. I've never hated you, Eva-bear. I loved you long before I should have, and the only way I managed to do the right thing was to push you away."

Eva gasped and jerked out of my grasp. "Love? A ring? Babies? Eight years?" Her head dropped forward, and her shoulders heaved as she took a series of deep breaths. "I'm so confused."

"Let me help you understand," I soothed before scooting off the bed, keeping her in my arms. Placing my feet flat on the ground, I pushed up and let Eva's legs fall and her body glide down mine until she was standing. "Wait right here," I commanded. Then I gave her a quick, hard kiss before striding into our spacious closet. I returned to her a moment later with two fluffy, blue robes in my hands. I helped her into one and quickly donned the other. Then I took her hand and led her down the hall to the only other room on this floor.

I pushed open the door and walked backward, my eyes staying glued to her face, not wanting to miss a single second of her reaction. Damn, I hoped I'd gotten it right.

Eva followed slowly, and when her eyes swept around the room, they became huge. She blinked owlishly, her mouth forming a little O, and her breath held in her lungs. Finally, she released a harsh exhale, and her shocked eyes landed on my face. "An art studio?"

"I will always do everything in my power to

make sure you have everything you ever wanted, Eva. This is our home, and I wanted you to have a space to do what you love. Somewhere that's yours, a sanctuary. If you want to keep working at the Met, I support that one hundred percent. It's one of the reasons I chose this penthouse. However, if you'd like to be home more and take on private restorations, now you have a space to do it."

Tears welled up in Eva's eyes, which gave me a moment of panic until she smiled so brightly that there was no need for the sun shining in from all of the windows. "Tucker," she breathed. "This is amazing. It's...perfect."

I smiled tenderly and took her hand again, leading her over to the table in the center of the room. Sitting in the center was a small, robin's egg blue box, and I picked it up before falling to one knee in front of Eva and flipping the lid.

"Eva Kendal, I love you more than anything. I've loved you for all of my life, though it has grown over the years from familial love, to young love, to forever love. I've waited all this time for you, my first love and my last. You've always been the only one for me, my own personal sun, shining light into every facet of my life. I can't live without you for one more day. I want to marry you, have a family with you, and grow old with you. Never again will you question my love for you because I will prove it over and over every single day for eternity." I removed the five-carat, emerald-cut platinum ring and slipped it onto her finger before placing a kiss on it. Then I stood and drew her into my arms, my head lowering so I could kiss her.

I was blocked from my goal by her hand covering my mouth. "Wait, didn't you forget something?" she asked with an arch look.

I frowned as I thought for a moment, then guessed, "I promise to give you endless amounts of orgasms?"

Eva giggled and shook her head. "I meant that you didn't ask me."

I raised a brow and stared down at her for a moment before responding. "No, I didn't."

"Well?" She put her hands on her hips, giving me an adorable little glare that made me want to kiss her and then press her up against the wall and fuck her. That suddenly became my new plan, and I wrapped my large hands around her arms, about to haul her into my body, but she broke the spell a second before our lips met. "Are you going to ask me?"

My head reared back, and I scowled at her.

"Fuck no," I scoffed. "That would imply that you have a choice. We're getting married, Eva." I placed my hand on her stomach and glanced down before returning my eyes to her face. "You could already be carrying our child, baby."

Eva's hands came to rest over mine, and the spark of wonder and joy in them shooed away any lingering doubts I might have had. I slowly walked her backward until she was pressed up against one of the sturdy glass walls and whispered, "How about we up those chances?" She started to say something, but it was muffled when my mouth crashed down over hers. I hoisted her up and guided her legs around my waist, holding her up with my hands under her luscious ass. I groaned when I felt her hot, wet pussy drenching my cock as I teased her opening with the tip while I continued to devour her mouth. She moaned but stiffened a little, making me pull back instantly. "Are you too sore, baby?" I'd taken her more than I probably should have the night before, considering she'd been a virgin. But every time I'd tried to pull back after getting a little carried away, she would cling to me and beg me not to stop. I didn't have the strength to deny her even though I knew she would probably be sore as fuck today.

She shook her head and bucked her hips, sucking

the fat tip of my dick inside her. "A little tender but not enough to stop. Fuck me, Tucker," she moaned.

To my surprise, I didn't have the desire to spank her—well, to be fair, I always wanted to spank her—for her language. Instead, a fire blazed inside me, burning my entire body from the inside out. Hearing her ask me to fuck her was sexy as hell and caused a spurt of come to escape my cock. "I should put you over my knee for that, baby," I growled. "But damn, that turned me the fuck on."

"Then do something about it," she demanded with a little wiggle that took even more of my shaft inside her.

"Anything you want, Eva-bear," I rasped before plunging the rest of the way in and slamming my mouth over hers, swallowing her scream of pleasure. I was half out of my mind and started to fuck her with deep, hard strokes. Every time her pussy clenched, massaging my dick, I fucked her even faster and harder. With one hand, I deftly untied her sash and pushed open the sides of her robe. With her tits exposed, I couldn't help tearing my mouth from hers and latching onto a rosy, peaked nipple.

Eva followed my example, and in seconds, my robe fell to the floor. She slid her palms up my chest, exploring the ridges of my muscles. Then she grasped my shoulders and her nails dug into the skin, pulling a low, ragged groan from my lips. I lost my fucking mind and began wildly rutting inside her like an animal, intent on breeding their mate.

Every time I pistoned inside her, she pumped her hips to meet me. The room was filled with grunts and moans, along with the sound of sweating skin slapping together. It was the most erotic thing I'd ever experienced, not that I really had other experience, but somehow, I knew what Eva and I had was special and unique.

"Tucker," Eva gasped. "I need—yes! Harder! Oh, yes! Tucker! Yes! Yes!" She chanted as I pushed her higher and higher, approaching the ledge I intended to toss her over into orgasmic oblivion. I slammed into her and hissed when her nails dug even deeper and her legs squeezed around my waist in a death grip. Drawing breath became a little more difficult, but who wouldn't want to die buried in their love's tight pussy?

"Fuck," I groaned. "I can barely get my cock out, baby. Your greedy little pussy doesn't want to let me go. You want me to come inside you, Eva? Give your body what it's begging for?"

Her head bobbed in a jerky up and down motion, and she whined with need. The tell-tale tingling at the base of my spine began to spread, and my balls were hanging heavy with what I had to give her. I'd been sucking and nibbling on both of her tits, but when I slipped a hand between us and pinched her swollen clit, I bit down on the bud in my mouth. It threw Eva over the edge, and she screamed my name as her pussy convulsed around my cock.

"Fuck, Eva! Oh, fuck, yeah! Fuck, baby! That's right, keep that pussy squeezing me. Fuck! " After a few more thrusts, I gave in to the demand of her pussy and let it suck my dick all the way in, holding me deep while I coated her womb with my thick cream. I dropped my head into the crook of her neck and sucked on her skin as my cock pulsed in rhythm with my rapidly beating heart.

My fingers continued to manipulate Eva's bundle of nerves, prolonging her orgasm as long as possible so her body would welcome every last drop of my come. Some of it was already leaking and dripping down my thighs. When her shudders subsided, I set her down and dropped to my knees, using her robe to clean her up a little. I went to wipe off my dick as well but the creamy coating of our mixed arousal shining on it had my cock swelling all over again. I fucking loved how it looked and what it meant.

"Tucker?" Eva's soft voice was hesitant, and I immediately shot to my feet to make sure she was okay.

"Are you alright?" I asked, my eyes doing a sweep of her naked body. "Did I hurt you?"

"No, no," she assured me hastily. "I was just wondering…" She trailed off, looking unsure, and I hated that she didn't feel comfortable opening up to me completely. But I knew we'd get there.

"You can ask me anything, Eva-bear."

She cleared her throat and blushed hard enough that I could see it through her already flushed skin. "You, um…you said you waited…?" Her face was practically tomato red, and though I wanted to laugh, I didn't want to embarrass her even more.

I knew what Eva was asking and decided to help her out. "Yes, Eva. I've never been with anyone but you. Even before I knew why, I couldn't bring myself to go on more than a couple of casual dates. So, yes. I've been waiting for you in every sense of the word."

Eva's lips parted, and she examined my face closely, most likely searching for a hint that I wasn't being sincere. She seemed to be satisfied with what she saw because a giant, blazing smile broke out on her face. It made my heart stop for a couple of beats.

She was so fucking gorgeous, and it blew my mind that I could call her mine.

As happy as I was at that moment, there was something I still needed. Even though I knew it, I wanted to hear her say the words. I clasped her cheeks in my palms and locked our eyes, making sure she could tell that I was able to see into her soul and would know if she lied. "Tell me you love me, Eva."

Her eyelids fell, and she coyly peered up at me through her lashes. "How do you know I love you?"

I glowered at her, silently telling her that I didn't appreciate her teasing. "Say it," I demanded again with a growl.

Eva inhaled slowly, and the wait nearly killed me. I was just about to fuck her and keep her from orgasming until she screamed it, when she purred, "I love you, Tucker Carrington. And even though you didn't ask, yes. I will marry you."

A weight I hadn't known I was carrying lifted, and I felt nothing but joy and love filling my soul. My body however, was filled with something else. I decided I wanted to hear her screaming her love for me anyway.

CHAPTER 7

TUCKER

A loud beep woke me from a dead sleep, and I jackknifed up in bed, startling Eva who'd been asleep on my chest. "Sorry, baby," I apologized softly. "Go back to sleep." I looked around for the offending noise but didn't see the source until I heard it again. There was an intercom on the wall, and it was blinking red. I glanced at the clock on the bedside table and saw that it was after two in the afternoon. I groaned, we'd only been asleep for an hour. I immediately knew who it was, and I grumbled as I climbed out of bed and padded over to the speaker. Twisting a knob, I turned the volume down before I pressed the microphone button.

"Yes?"

"Good day, Tucker," Kendra chirped. Exhausted

from spending the morning between my fiancée's legs, I glared at Kendra even though I knew she couldn't see me.

"Who the hell is that?" Eva snapped.

My head whipped around to see Eva kneeling on the bed with her hands on her hips, staring at me with furrowed brows and her mouth twisted as though she'd been sucking on lemons. The daggers in her eyes made me want to laugh. Her jealousy was adorable and sexy as hell, but I had a feeling that if I so much as snickered, she'd go after my balls. And I needed those to knock my girl up...among other reasons.

"It's our housekeeper, baby," I explained, trying to ignore her bouncing tits as she breathed heavily. As well as the mouthwatering sight of her naked mound, that had me licking my lips in anticipation.

"Who are you...do you have a girl here, Tucker Carrington?" Kendra gasped. Shit, that got my attention away from Eva's gorgeous, naked body. I'd left my finger on the speaker button. I almost groaned, knowing that Kendra's comment probably sounded like a jealous girlfriend rather than a flabbergasted housekeeper.

Eva's eyes narrowed even more, and I rushed to

explain. "Kendra's been with me for years, Eva-bear, and she's like a second mother to me."

"Eva!" Kendra shrieked through the speaker. "*The* Eva?"

My girl's expression softened a little, and I breathed a small sigh of relief. "Was there something you needed, Kendra?" I asked, failing to keep the exasperation out of my tone.

"I need to meet this woman who's had you tied up in knots and—"

"Anything else?" I snapped, interrupting her before she forced a discussion between me and Eva that I wasn't ready to have.

"Would you and your guest like some lunch, Mr. Carrington?"

Fuck. I was going to pay for my attitude, but I mentally shrugged. If I was already in trouble with Kendra... "Yes, please. Oh, and Kendra?"

"Yes, sir?" I rolled my eyes at the moniker. Yeah, I was definitely in deep shit with her.

"Tell Anthony he doesn't have to sneak out the back entrance. He can use the front door."

I turned off the intercom completely and chuckled as I turned around, then sighed. Eva was sitting now, holding a sheet in front of her, shielding my view of her big, delicious tits.

Eva shook her head and smirked. "She's going to spit in your food, naughty boy."

My long legs ate up the distance to the bed, and I grinned wickedly as I got on the mattress and crawled over her, forcing her onto her back. I dipped one finger into the valley between her tits and drew the sheet away. "I can be much naughtier, baby," I purred as I leered at her.

She squirmed, and if I wasn't so aware of my Eva, I might have missed the tiny wince. I gulped and pushed back my growing desire. "How about a bath before lunch?" I suggested, allowing myself one more touch and running a finger along her jaw, down her neck, and over one breast. The little catch in her breath when the pad of my finger glided over her nipple almost broke my resolve to give her body a break.

"Are you going to take it with me?" she asked with a saucy smile.

I laughed at how fucking adorable she was but shook my head with genuine regret. "I've ridden you hard since last night"—Eva smirked and opened her mouth, but I pressed a finger over it, knowing she was about to make a smartass comment about riding me—"even though I knew better. Your body needs rest, or you won't be able to walk for a few days. And if I get into that bath with you—" I broke off and shook my head. "You'll be walking funny for a week."

Eva pouted, but I ignored it as I lifted her into my arms and strode to the bathroom. Once she was settled in a warm bath, I took a quick shower and scurried from the room before I gave in to temptation. It was especially difficult with Eva constantly looking at my body with heated eyes. Careful of the hard on I was sporting, I pulled on a pair of jeans and donned a T-shirt. Dressed, I jogged down the stairs to the first floor, making my way into the kitchen.

Kendra was standing at the counter with her back to me, setting a plate with a sandwich onto an already full tray of food. I stealthily came up behind her and gave her a quick hug. She screamed and whirled around, her hand flying to her chest.

"You know I love you, right?" I asked with a boyish smile.

She glared at me for a moment, then sighed and shook her head, clearly exasperated. "I should have poisoned your food, but I can't be mad when you look this happy." I grinned and smacked a kiss on her cheek. "So," she asked, "are you going to let her out of the bedroom so I can meet her?"

I pretended to consider my options but was startled when she gasped, "Tucker, please tell me you didn't actually kidnap Eva and have her tied up in the bedroom!"

Even though she was partly right, I doubled over with laughter. If she'd been wearing pearls, she probably would have been clutching them as she crossed herself and said a prayer for my soul. I felt the smack of what was probably a wooden spoon on my shoulder, and it only made me laugh harder.

"For some reason, I wouldn't be surprised if tying me up and holding me hostage was Tucker's backup plan if I hadn't agreed to marry him."

Kendra and I both looked at the door to see Eva standing there looking fresh and clean with her hair piled on top of her head and wearing one of my shirts. It was a good thing it came all the way to her knees, or else I would have marched her sexy little ass back upstairs to change. I didn't care if it was a woman; nobody was allowed to see what belonged to me and only me. As it was, my cock sprang to life at the sight of my girl wearing my clothes. I'd stocked our closet with everything a girl could need, but now I was considering burning everything so she would have no choice but to wear my clothes all of the time.

Kendra rushed over to Eva and pulled her into a big hug. "I'm so happy to meet you, Eva!" she gushed. "I was starting to worry that my boy would never man up and go after you. I didn't want to see him grow into a lonely, grumpy old man."

Eva giggled and hugged her back, a beautiful smile gracing her face. "I'm surprised he even talked about me."

I briefly wondered if it would be too suspicious if I snatched up Eva and ran upstairs to lock her away before Kendra could reveal my secret. She was the only one, outside of my dad, who knew about the level of my obsession with Eva.

"He didn't actually," Kendra began, causing Eva's brow to wrinkle with confusion. "It was all—"

"I'm glad you two were able to meet," I said loudly, cutting Kendra off. I grabbed the tray of food in one arm before stalking over to Eva and tucking her into my side. "Thanks for lunch. We've got plans, so we'll eat while we get ready." Then I dragged Eva to the elevator and headed back to the bedroom.

We were both starving, so I managed to avoid any questions while we devoured our food. Once we'd finished, I cleared away the dishes and the tray, setting them on a dumbwaiter that went down to the pantry and hit the button to start its descent.

"We have an appointment," I told Eva as I crossed

the room and entered the closet. The personal shopper had followed my instructions perfectly, so I was able to grab the outfit I wanted without taking the time to hunt it down. A pretty white summer dress was on the hanger with a clear bag that contained shoes, jewelry, and a hair clip that had belonged to my mother.

"What's going...?" Eva had followed me into the closet, but when she stepped inside, she stopped and gasped. "Holy sh—crap!" She looked around, her face a mask of wonder and awe. "This is like my dream closet on steroids." I laughed but caught her arm as she started to walk around.

"You can explore to your heart's content later," I told her with a wink. "Right now, you need to change so we aren't late." I handed her the outfit I'd chosen and turned her around, then patted her bum to get her moving toward the bathroom.

"Late to what?" she asked over her shoulder.

"You'll see," I answered evasively. I wasn't sure how easy this was going to go, but one way or another, I was going to be making love to my wife tonight.

I put on a suit and figured I'd wait in my office, but when I opened the bathroom door to tell Eva, I was shocked to see that she was ready to go and almost knocked on my ass by how fucking gorgeous she was.

"Put your eyes and tongue back in your head, Tucker," she teased as she sauntered toward me. "This dress is stunning, and if it's for what I think it is, I don't want you ruining it by trying to get me out of it."

If I wasn't desperate to have Eva legally tied to me in every way, I might have pouted. Which was ridiculous. I didn't pout. I wasn't a child being denied its favorite toy. Although the situation was strikingly similar...

After a few deep breaths to calm my body down—not very successfully—I laced my fingers with Eva's and led her toward her future.

CHAPTER 8

TUCKER

"My mom and dad are going to be so mad," Eva moaned as we walked into the office to file our paperwork. She hadn't made any objections to my plan for us to get married tonight, but she'd been fretting over her family's reaction. "Trevor and my dad just might kill you, Tucker." I chuckled when I glanced at her face and saw the very real worry there. "I'm serious, Tucker!" she whisper-yelled since we were the next in line.

A college-age, hipster-type guy sat behind the desk looking bored until we stepped up to the window. His eyes were covered by round, red-framed glasses, but they didn't hide the way his gaze swept over Eva, lingering on her chest. I growled and leaned down, getting in the pipsqueak's now frightened face. "Those glasses won't stop me from blackening both of your eyes if you don't stop staring at my woman." He swallowed hard and put his head down.

"Don't be such a caveman," Eva scolded.

I narrowed my eyes, and my arm tightened around her. "You're mine, Eva. I don't give a fuck if it makes me a caveman. I don't want other men looking at you as though they're picturing you naked. That image belongs to me alone."

Eva rolled her eyes, but she couldn't hide the heat that flared in their blue depths or the pleased little smile that curved her lips. Yeah, she didn't want to admit it, but obviously my possessiveness made her hot. Which was fine by me because I could guarantee it wasn't going to get any better.

As we walked away, I returned to our previous conversation. "I already asked your dad and brother for permission to marry you, Eva-bear," I said as I tucked her into my side and kissed her temple.

I thought she would be relieved and relax, but I was proven wrong when she poked me in the side and hissed, "That's great, but who is going to protect you from my mom when she realizes that she wasn't at my wedding?"

I certainly wasn't looking forward to facing Blair after this, but ultimately, it didn't matter. I would do anything to have Eva, and until she was legally mine, I would mow down any obstacle in my way. Better to ask for forgiveness than permission.

I'd called in a favor from a judge who I'd helped out of a jam, and after getting our paperwork squared away, I led Eva down to his chambers. He called for us to enter after one knock and when we walked inside, he stood and gave us a friendly smile. When he greeted Eva, his hands and eyes didn't linger, which made me like the guy even more. I wouldn't have brought my fiancée to him if I didn't know he was happily married and loved to boast about his children and grandchildren.

I shook his hand and thanked him for doing this on short notice, but before I could say more, there was a knock on the door. Eva gasped when it opened, and her mother walked inside, followed by her father and my parents.

Blair rushed over to Eva, and I had to fight the urge to drag her into my arms to make sure no one tried to take her away. I focused my energy on my dad instead, who held up his hands and stepped back. "It was Kendra, I swear."

My mom stomped up to me and went up to the very tip of her toes to smack the side of my head. "Ouch," I grumbled, rubbing the sting away.

"You deserve a whole lot more, Tucker Carrington," she snapped. "Not inviting me to your wedding? Why wouldn't you want me here?" Her eyes filled with tears, and I suddenly felt two inches tall. Shit. I hated it when my mom cried. I looked at my dad for help, but he just glared at me, silently ordering me to fix it.

I wrapped my mom up in a bear hug and kissed her cheek. "Of course, I wanted you here, Mom. I was just...we were in a hurry and—"

Eva scoffed, and I threw her a pleading glance, mouthing that I loved her. After a minute, she sighed and saved my ass. "I'm sorry. Mom, Penny, I swear we didn't do this to shut you out." Eva's eyes met mine, and she gave me a tiny smirk, her eyes dancing with wicked mirth. I had a feeling I'd been wrong; Eva wasn't saving me, she was throwing me to the wolves...without getting me arrested for kidnapping. "I'm pregnant, and we didn't want to have the baby out of wedlock."

Son of a bitch. She'd handed my ass over to her dad on a silver platter. I didn't know what it said about me that it made her even sexier. Her intelligence and strength were as hot as her delectable body. She winked at me, clearly following the path of my thoughts and wiggled her ass a little more than necessary when she turned around and walked over to a small sitting area and took a seat. She had definitely earned herself a thorough spanking when we got home.

"You're what?" Blair gasped at the same time that Justice shouted, "What the fuck?"

My dad groaned and dropped into the nearest chair, shaking his head, mumbling something about me being too much like my old man. If I hadn't been so angry and frustrated by the whole situation, I might have laughed because it was true. I didn't see that as a bad thing, however.

Unlike everyone else, my mom was ecstatic, and she clapped while bouncing on the balls of her feet excitedly. "A baby!"

The cacophony of sound was giving me a headache, and I was about out of patience in regard to my wedding.

"Quiet!" I shouted. Then I addressed all the parents as a group. "First of all, Eva and I are adults. We don't have to ask permission to get married or have a baby, or anything else we decide to do as a couple. We are getting married. This isn't up for discussion." I held up my hand when Justice started to speak and was a little astonished when he backed off for the moment. "That being said, we love and respect you all, and I know I speak for Eva when I tell you that we are truly sorry for not telling you about this and are very happy that you're here now."

Eva stood and ran over to throw herself into my arms, almost bowling me over. "I love you," she exclaimed as she hugged me tight. Everyone but her faded away, and I bent low to brush my lips over hers.

"I love you too, Eva-bear. How's about we get hitched?"

She laughed and kissed me a little harder before stepping back and lifting her chin stubbornly. Then she pivoted on her heel to face her parents. "I love Tucker. We're getting married. I'm so happy you're here, but if you have a problem with it, now's the time to leave."

Justice grumbled, but I spotted the pride in his eyes as he gazed at his daughter. Blair started crying, but she had a big smile on her face. "Oh, honey," she sniffled. "You're all grown up. And now my baby is having a baby..."

"Tucker," Justice's voice was a low growl, and a lesser man would probably have shriveled up and died under his dark glare. "You knocked up my daughter before marrying her?"

Eva looked up at me guiltily, but I just shook my head, silently telling her to let me handle this.

"Sir, you know I had every intention of marrying your daughter. I could understand your anger if I hadn't already asked for her hand. But I respect you, and Trevor, too much to have ever married Eva without doing so. And since I did come to you, and received your blessing, I fail to see how it matters when Eva and I choose to have children. That is a decision we make as a couple. And Blair, Mom...I promise, you can throw Eva the wedding of her dreams later, but we're getting married now."

Eva sighed, and when I glanced down to check on her, I was captivated by the love shining from her eyes and turned on by the way she was looking dreamily at me, like I was her hero. But now wasn't the time, so I turned my focus back to Eva's parents. I was relieved to see a touch of admiration in their expressions. Though Justice still didn't look all that happy about the situation.

Blair's eyes were teary as she stared at Eva, and she smiled softly when she said, "Honey, you look so beautiful. And...really happy."

"I am, Mom," Eva answered, and I could've sworn that I actually heard her smile in her voice.

"Tucker loves me the way Dad loves you. And the way Jonah loves Penny."

If we'd been alone, I would have stripped Eva bare and worshipped every inch of her body. She'd just given me the highest compliment I could ever receive. My patience officially ran out at that moment. I turned to the judge, who'd been quietly sitting at his desk the whole time, clearly enjoying the drama. "We're getting married now," I demanded in more of a statement than a request. He grinned and jumped to his feet.

Our parents came to stand at our sides, and I was grateful they were there. But the only thing I would remember from that ceremony was how fucking gorgeous my bride was and the feeling of utter bliss when she said, "I do."

∼

I WALKED into the restoration room at the Met and frowned as I prowled toward the table where my wife was bent over her latest project. A young guy was hovering near her, standing a little too close for my liking. As I approached, I could hear what he was saying, and the way his eyes were glued to her chest had fury building inside me.

"You're so talented, Eva. Maybe we could go to lunch sometime, and you can tell me about—" he broke off and his head whipped in my direction when I growled.

"Did you miss the fucking giant diamond on her hand?" I snarled.

He backed away a few steps and shook his head. "I didn't mean—I thought maybe Eva—"

He took another step back, and I glared as I jerked my head toward the room's exit. "I suggest you run along, boy. *Mrs. Carrington*"—I emphasized her name through gritted teeth—"is going to lunch with her man." The kid swallowed hard before nodding and hotfooting it out of my sight.

When I turned to my wife, she was looking up at me and rolled her eyes. "He was harmless, you crazy caveman."

I narrowed my eyes and cupped her elbow to help her to her feet so I could wrap her up in my embrace. "He was hitting on another man's wife." I blew out a harsh breath and raised my eyes to the ceiling. "I figured once I had my ring on your finger, I'd be done scaring off assholes who're sniffing around you."

"What are you talking about?" Eva's tone brought my gaze back to her face. She was watching me with suspicion. I tried to smile innocently, but it backfired because she only seemed even more distrustful. I searched for something to say, a way to explain away my comment, but came up blank. "Tucker Carrington," she hissed, "were you the reason I couldn't get a second date in high school?"

I cleared my throat and glanced around; this was not the place to have this conversation. "Let's go home and I'll make you some lunch," I cajoled with my most charming smile.

Eva looked as though she was about to argue, but then she looked around as well and simply nodded. I helped her don her jacket, then took her hand as we made our way to the exit.

Once we arrived home, I guided her to one of the islands in the kitchen and boosted her up onto a stool. She was quiet while I gathered the ingredients to make her favorite cold pasta salad. Finally, she broke the silence. "Don't think making my favorite food and looking all sexy while doing it is going to get you out of this discussion, Tucker," she announced.

"Fuck," I sighed in a low enough voice that she didn't hear it. "Yes, I ran off the punks you chose to date in high school," I admitted, a little louder. "In my defense," I quickly added, "you were always choosing spineless little shits."

"I think I owe Trevor an apology," she mused before her head snapped up, and she glared at me. "What do you mean I picked the wrong guys?"

"First, not one of those little fuckers fought for you," I explained as I finished up her lunch and set a bowl of pasta in front of her. "Second, if I hadn't done it, Trevor or Justice would have." Yeah, I was throwing my best friend and surrogate uncle under the bus, and I didn't feel a second of guilt. Mostly because it was true.

Eva gasped. "Even my dad knew?"

I grinned and nodded. "Pretty sure it gained me some brownie points for when I told them I was going to marry you."

"I'm going to kill them," she muttered as she shoveled a bite in her mouth and moaned.

I clenched my jaw and grabbed to the edge of the island, squeezing so hard that my knuckles turned white. Being married for three months hadn't done shit to help my raging desire for my wife, and that little sound had me fighting the need to lay her out on the counter and eat her pussy until she was screaming my name.

"It's in the past, baby—"

"Wait." Eva interrupted me, her head cocked to the side, and her face adorably screwed up in concentration. "You left for London the summer before my junior year, and...it didn't stop after high school." Her eyes found mine, and I considered going for innocent again, but what was the point? I wasn't ashamed of what I'd done to protect Eva, or the lengths I went to in order to make sure that she would always be mine. I shrugged and leaned my elbows on the counter, bringing our faces inches apart. "I told you, baby. I was never far from you."

"B-but...you were in London," she sputtered.

I grinned and winked at her. "It's amazing what money can buy. My eyes were always on you in some way or another. I have always and will always protect what's mine."

"Eyes? Like bodyguards and stuff?" She wrinkled her nose in such a cute way that I had to place a kiss on the tip.

"Yes." I was about to confess to the cameras and hacking to security feeds but thought better of it after a moment. She didn't need to know every single detail, right? Nor did I think it was the best time to confess that I still had eyes on her all the time. "Among other things," I hedged. "Eva-bear, you are what I live for. The reason I keep breathing. If I hadn't been close to you in some way, I would have lost my fucking mind. And if any man had touched you—" I break off and ball my hands into fists and growled, my mind imagining the painful death of any motherfucker who dared to lay a finger on my Eva.

She sighed and shook her head, but her cheeks bloomed with pink and the corners of her lips curved up. "Such a caveman," she muttered as she went back to eating. When she didn't say anything more, I raised a brow and watched her in silence. She eventually looked up from her food and smiled at my questioning expression. "I know your level of obsession with me could probably be considered unhealthy." The flush of her skin darkened, and her eyes flashed with heat. "And I know I shouldn't, but for some reason, I think it's sexy as fuck."

"Language, baby," I gritted in reprimand. Although the rigid nature of my muscles wasn't from anger, I was trying to keep myself from losing complete control and fucking her like an animal on the kitchen floor.

"Oops." She didn't look the least bit contrite.

I stalked around the island until I was standing between her thighs. My hands palmed her ass, and I yanked her forward, pressing my hard cock against her pussy. "Are you trying to get yourself a blistered ass, Eva-bear?" It turned my girl wild when I spanked her ass or her pussy. Which could have made it a less effective punishment, but when I turned her tender globes bright red, she felt it every time she sat down the next day. Still, she liked to provoke me and knew exactly how to push my buttons.

Eva's legs curled around the backs of my thighs, and her arms went around my neck, pillowing her perfect tits against my chest. She buried her face in my neck, and a second later, I felt the sting of a bite. "Maybe," she whispered.

I was suddenly starving. "Are you done eating, baby?" I rasped as all of the blood in my body rushed south. She nodded, causing her silky hair to get caught in my scruff. "Good. My turn." I carried her out of the kitchen and up to our bedroom where I spent the next several hours feasting until I was sated. I knew I would never have my fill of her, but it wouldn't stop me from trying.

EPILOGUE

EVA

One year later

Our moms had quickly taken Tucker up on his offer to plan the wedding of my dreams. They were so excited that they'd gotten right to work on it the same day we got married. They'd been forced to wait a year to pull it off, though, because the little joke I'd pulled on Tucker when we got married turned out to be prophetic when we realized I'd gotten pregnant right away. Not that it was much of a surprise, considering how many times my husband pumped his come into me.

Since I'd refused to have my fancier—but not

more romantic because nothing could top the moment Tucker stood up to my dad at the courthouse—wedding with a rounded belly, we decided to make it a vow renewal for our one-year anniversary. It was a good thing we hadn't put it off any longer because I had one heck of an anniversary present for my sexy hubby, and I couldn't wait to share it with him. But first, we had to get through this round of toasts before we could take the dance floor for our first "official" dance as a married couple.

My father-in-law stood and winked at us before beginning. "When I first realized my oldest son was falling for Eva"—Tucker's frantic expression made me giggle because I knew he was freaked out by the possibility that my dad and brother would realize exactly how young I'd been—"I was a little worried about how it might impact the bond between our families if their relationship didn't work out."

Tucker leveled a glare at his dad, making me giggle because of how ridiculous it was for him to be pissed at Jonah's toast. Leaning deeper into his side, I whispered, "Relax, babe. We've more than proved that we're meant to be together."

"Damn straight," Tucker muttered under his breath.

"I wasn't concerned for long, though. Not after

I realized that my son looked at Eva the same way I look at my wife." Jonah's gaze slid down and to the side, and the love he felt for Penelope shone brightly from his eyes, even after all the years they'd been together. "Then I knew there wasn't any chance of them breaking up because Tucker wouldn't ever let her go. He takes after his dad, after all."

"And his father-in-law," my mom tossed in, making the crowd laugh. My dad chuckled and shook his head, but it wasn't as though he could deny how crazy he was about my mom. Everyone knew how he was with her.

"For sure," I agreed with a grin. "When you really think about it, Dad only has himself to blame for me falling for Tucker. He's the only guy who could ever live up to the example my dad set for what I wanted in a husband."

"And he'd better keep living up to it or else," Dad grumbled as he straightened in his seat and threw Tucker a warning glance.

"There's no need to threaten the boy," my mom chided, patting my dad's arm before twisting in her seat to reach into the stroller where my daughter slept. She gently ran her fingers through my daughter's fine, blond hair, being careful not to wake her since she'd only drifted off five minutes ago. "He's as protective of his girls as you are of our family."

"Sometimes, I think he might even be worse with me than you are with Mom," I half-teased, knowing my dad would never believe it even though he'd seen with his own eyes how Tucker had hovered over me every moment of my pregnancy.

"Good." My dad nodded in approval, his lips curving up in a pleased smile.

My mom sighed as I rolled my eyes, but Tucker smiled back at my dad. Before I could tease him about the male-bonding moment—one that made me happy because I loved knowing that the two most important men in my life got along so well—the DJ announced that it was time for the dance I'd been waiting all night for.

Tucker led me to the dance floor and tugged me close to his body. One of his hands cupped my hip and the other tangled in my hair at the back of my head. Bending his head to my ear, he asked, "Do you think they realize we've danced together before?"

Thinking about how perfect we moved together when we were horizontal—and sometimes vertical too, like in the shower this morning—I waggled my eyebrows at him. "Considering we gave our parents a grandchild barely nine months after we got married,

I'm pretty sure they know we've done the horizontal mambo."

Tucker laughed and pulled me closer to his body, pressing his hard length against my belly. "I can't wait until I have you all to myself in our hotel suite where we'll have the whole night together without any interruptions."

My parents were staying two floors below us so they could watch the baby. At fourteen weeks old, it was the first night she wasn't spending with us, and my mom had known I'd want her nearby. But she didn't know the other reason I'd wanted it to be just the two of us tonight. Tucker was going to be the first to know, and it was finally the perfect moment to share the news. "It's a good thing we didn't put today off any longer."

"Why's that, baby?" Tucker asked as he pressed a kiss to the top of my head.

I wrapped my hand around his wrist and tugged his hand until it rested over my belly. "If we'd waited too much longer, my dress wouldn't have fit."

He stopped right there on the dance floor, his dark eyes filled with incandescent joy. "You're pregnant?"

I nodded, unable to get words past the lump of emotion in my throat. He lifted me and twirled me around in a circle before gently setting me on my feet. Turning toward where our family and friends were still seated, he shouted, "We're having another baby!"

Everyone rushed over to offer their congratulations, but Tucker only waited a few minutes before he tugged me toward the door. "We can't just leave," I insisted, dragging my feet a bit in an attempt to slow our progress.

Tucker bent down to slide his arm under my knees and lifted me into his arms. "Everyone else can stay as late as they want, but we're done. It's past time for us to celebrate by ourselves."

I wrapped my arms around his neck and laid my head against his shoulder. I couldn't argue when he was giving me exactly what I wanted—just like he always did.

EPILOGUE

TUCKER

6 years later

"Spread those legs wide, baby," I commanded as I buried my face in my wife's soaked pussy. My thumbs held her lips open, exposing her pink and swollen center, her little clit peeking out and begging for my mouth. I licked the hard bud, and Eva's hips bucked up as she let out a little scream.

I slapped one ass cheek with the flat of my palm and growled, "Quiet, Eva-bear. If you wake the baby, I won't be able to make you come."

Eva whimpered, but I could tell that she was

pressing her lips together, trying to contain her sounds of pleasure. "Good girl," I praised softly before diving back in to lap at her cream. I fucking loved to hear my woman screaming my name, but it wasn't something we could do with four little cock-blockers running around or sleeping one floor below.

She tensed, and her body began to shake. My eyes lifted in time to see her smash a pillow over her face, muffling her scream as she squirted into my mouth. I groaned as I drank every drop until her shudders subsided.

When she was limp and panting, I crawled up her body and wrapped her legs around me. I kissed her, swallowing her moan as she tasted herself on my lips. My hands cupped her tits—swollen from nursing our youngest baby—and squeezed them. Though it seemed impossible, I hardened even more when the white droplets beaded on her big, rosy red nipples. Groaning, I licked each tip before sucking one into my mouth as I slammed inside her. My balls slapped against her ass when I bottomed out, and I muttered, "Fuck. So damn tight." Licking and nibbling her nipples, I began to move. Slow at first but quickly gaining speed as I felt my control fading away. Eva's nails bit into the skin of my shoulders and she pressed her lips to my chest to keep from making noise.

The bed squeaked with the force of my thrusts, and if the headboard hadn't been mounted to the wall, it would have been banging against it. That was a lesson we learned after our first baby was woken one too many times from the pounding.

"Harder, Tucker," Eva breathed. "Fuck me harder."

I pulled out and glared at Eva before flipping her to her stomach and lifting her ass in the air. The sharp crack of my hand meeting her ass was the only sound in the room besides our heavy breathing. I gently pushed Eva's head down until her face was pressed into the mattress, containing her cries as I slapped each cheek until she was pink and her arousal was dripping down her thighs. Then I shoved my cock back into her heat, and the scream that ripped from her throat was barely audible, but loud enough to send fire racing down my spine, straight to my cock. I threw my head back and clenched my jaw to keep from roaring as I spilled inside her, filling her with my thick, heavy cream. I pumped in and out lazily, prolonging our orgasms as much as possible and watched my cock disappear and reappear covered in the sweet mix of our come. It was almost enough to have my slightly softened cock become rock hard again.

Eva collapsed, and I removed my hand from the back of her head so she could turn it to the side and breathe easier. "Holy cow," she sighed. "When's the last time we've gone this long during sex without an interruption?" A small laugh shook her shoulders and I chuckled along with her as I dropped down to rest beside her.

I gathered her into my arms and sighed. "I don't know," I answered. "But, it's probably the last time I was able to hear you scream my name without a pillow or mattress muffling you." The thought caused me to harden completely, and Eva wiggled a little when she felt my cock poking her ass. I gripped her hips and held her still. "Stop, baby. Unless you're ready to have my monster cock fucking your tight pussy again." We'd gone three rounds already, and I'd ridden her hard. The flu had hit our kids, and it had been thirty-eight hours and seventeen minutes since I'd been inside my wife. I was backed up. "You're already going to be sore in the morning," I mumbled into her hair. "If I get inside you again, you might not be able to walk."

She sighed and snuggled deeper into my embrace. "Worth it."

I snickered and kissed her head. The alarm on my phone buzzed, and I glanced at the clock to see that it was midnight. *Finally.* I gently turned Eva onto her back and placed a soft kiss on her bee-stung lips. "Happy birthday, Eva-bear."

Her face broke out into a bright smile, and she cupped her hands together, waiting expectantly. It was so fucking cute that I couldn't contain my hearty laughter. My wife knew me well. I'd never been able to last past the first minute of her birthday before giving her a gift.

I gave her a confused glance and volleyed my eyes back and forth between her face and empty hands. "What? Is there something you want?" I teased.

She glared at me and poked me in the chest before holding out her hands once more. "Where's my present?"

"Fuck, I love you." I kissed her, and when I released her lips, she looked dazed for a moment, then the fog cleared, and she raised a single eyebrow. I laughed again while I reached over her to open the drawer in my nightstand.

"I love you too," she replied. Then she wiggled her fingers. "Present."

I dropped a flat, rectangular box into her waiting

hands, and she beamed at me. "Speaking of screaming orgasms..." I said with a smirk.

Eva's canted her head to the side and eyed me curiously before attacking the box. Inside were two plane tickets and a bill of sale. She lifted the bill of sale first, and her mouth formed a little O, her eyes growing wide. "You bought an island?" she shrieked before slapping a hand over her mouth.

"I decided that we needed a place of our own for a little 'adult' time," I elucidated with a grin. "Somewhere you can be as loud as you want, and I won't need to kill anyone for hearing what's mine alone." She rolled her eyes, but the smile on her face was blinding. I brushed her messy blond hair back from her face and kissed her tenderly. "My parents are taking the kids for a week. We'll leave this afternoon." I winked. "So you see, you might want to be able to walk tomorrow."

Eva snickered and threw the box and its contents to the floor before flinging her arms around my neck. She kissed me with such raw passion that I was helpless to fight my growing need, and when she climbed onto my lap, lowering her hot, naked pussy onto my steel rod, my control snapped.

"Walking is overrated," she panted a while later as I fell onto the bed beside her. My heart felt like it was going to beat right out of my chest. "You'll be there to carry me."

With my last ounce of energy, I curled myself around my wife and cuddled her close. "Always."

Next up in this series is Only Love! We also have more coming soon in our Vegas, Baby series! And if you sign up for our newsletter, you'll get an email from us with a link to claim a free copy of The Virgin's Guardian, which is no longer available on Amazon.

ABOUT THE AUTHOR

The writing duo of Elle Christensen and Rochelle Paige team up under the Fiona Davenport pen name to bring you sexy, insta-love stories filled with alpha males. If you want a quick & dirty read with a guaranteed happily ever after, then give Fiona Davenport a try!

Don't miss out on new release news and giveaways; sign up for our newsletter!